THE LEGEND OF
ORVIS RAY

Written
by
Melody
Loyola

Illustrated
by
Leo
Loyola

love others well

ISBN-13: 978-1-73091-300-6

This book is dedicated to my grandmother, Lottie B. Wilson, who, by her example, taught all of us to love others well.

Orvis Ray had a great big smile.

If you met him, he'd say "Hi-dee!
How you?"

And would shake your hand. Or give
you a big hug.

And you would always feel loved.

He was born a long time ago, in the country, on a farm

Where the grass was the greenest of green

And the pond was as clear as glass

And the chickens and cows made happy noises.

He lived with his Mama and Daddy, big brother and little sister in a little house.

Life was good for Orvis Ray.

But one day, Orvis Ray got sick.

And though his family cared for
him and prayed,

And the doctor who came to visit
did all he could,

Orvis Ray was never the same.

It was really hard for him to learn.

And when he talked, it was hard to understand him.

But that didn't matter, because he
always felt loved.
And Orvis Ray loved everyone.

He didn't go to school very long.

And he couldn't read or write.

But that didn't matter.

He knew about everything by
talking with people

He would wave to a neighbor and say,
"Hi-dee! How you?"

And he would talk and talk about his day.
And he would ask about theirs.

But even though it was hard to
understand him,

Orvis Ray always made them feel special.

And he grew to be a big,
strong man.

He worked hard in the field,
hauling hay.

He could pitch a bale of hay a
mile high!

He couldn't take a driving test
to get a license,
but that didn't matter.

Sometimes he got to drive the
truck or a tractor in the fields
and that was fun.

And he never hit a cow, or
any people.

And when he was finished, he was hungry.

At supper time, he could eat a whole loaf of bread

or a dozen dinner rolls

and all his other food, too!!!

But when he wasn't working,

he liked to spend time at the town square.

And when he would see someone walk by,

he would say, "Hi-dee! How you?"

and he would ask them, "How's your
Mama" or "How's your boy?"—and smile.

Sometimes he would go to a basketball or football game or rodeo.

He loved to roller skate every Friday night and go bowling with his church friends.

And when he was there,
he would say,

"Hi-dee! How you?"

to each and every person
he met and smile.

And sometimes he would
give them a hug.

On Wednesdays and Sundays, he loved to go to church and he loved to sing.

He couldn't read the words to the song, so he hummed right along in tune with the others.

And when he was there, he would talk to his friends.

Orvis Ray couldn't read the local newspaper, but that didn't matter.

He knew all the news because he talked to people.

He would say, "Hi-dee! How you?"

"How's your Daddy?" "How's your bru-brah?" "My birf-day comin'!" and smile.

When people moved away from his small town and came back,

they would see Orvis Ray sitting on the town square

and he would say, "Hi-dee! How you?" and smile.

And they would know they were home.

Some people say
that Orvis Ray
never met a
stranger

and never forgot
a face.

He was
interested to
know everybody

and talk to them.

And every time
they saw him,
they felt loved.

So when you are out and about and see someone,

Just remember to show love like Orvis Ray.

Say "Hi-dee! How are you?" and
find out how they are doing.

LOVE
OTHERS
WELL!

THE END

About the author and illustrator:

Melody Loyola is a non-profit executive who enjoys traveling, learning about different cultures, and cooking.

Leo Loyola is an Episcopal priest with an incredible, life-long knack for drawing.

The couple loves spending time with their son.

40312410R00020

Made in the USA
Columbia, SC
12 December 2018